You Know It!

SAMMY
the Steiger

Gotcha!

FRANKIE
the Farmall

CODY
the Combine

Hey Dudes!

BAILEY
the Baler

Go Team!

KELLIE
the Combine

Awesome!

PETER
the Patriot Sprayer

VROOM!

SCOOTER
the CIH Scout

Let's Do It!

TAMMI
the Tiller

Details!

EVAN
the Early-Riser Planter

A Year on the Farm

with Casey & Friends

Happy Skies Farm

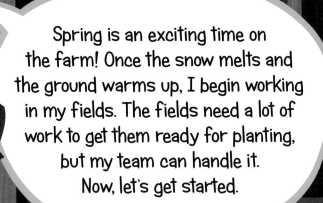

Spring is an exciting time on the farm! Once the snow melts and the ground warms up, I begin working in my fields. The fields need a lot of work to get them ready for planting, but my team can handle it. Now, let's get started.

Casey plans for the entire year, but there are some things she can't predict—like the weather. If the spring is too cold or rainy, Casey may not be able to plant new crops when she wants to. That can cause problems throughout the rest of the growing season. The crops need to be planted at just the right moment so they have time to grow big and strong. Hopefully this year, the weather will work with us!

Let's Till!

Each spring, the first thing I do is till the fields. Tilling is the action of digging into the ground and breaking up the soil into small chunks. When the soil is broken up, water and food can easily reach the seeds that I will plant. Farmers like me call that a good growing environment!

Hi there! My name is Tammi, and I'm in charge of tilling. My strong "fingers" break up the hard ground as Sammy pulls me up and down the fields. Together, we get the job done!

That's right, Tammi, we work as a team! I'm Sammy, the most powerful tractor on the farm. It is hard work pulling Tillie, so it's good that I'm strong.

Look at me till that field!

TILLUS TALK

Happy Plants Need a Good Home.

Tilling turns hard soil into a good soft home for seeds.

Hard soil acts like a brick. It does not let water, air, or plant food pass through it.

Soft soil acts like a sponge. It soaks up water, air, and plant food.

SIZE 'EM UP

	13' 0"
	5'10"
	4'3"
	6"

Time to Plant!

Now that the soil is tilled, it's time for me to plant seeds so they can grow. Planting the seeds by hand would take a long time. Instead, I use a machine called a "planter" to do the work for me!

My name is Evan, and I plant the seeds. I work quickly and carefully! I believe that every seed counts!

I'm Big Red! I pull Evan up and down the fields while he works. Planting is a big job, but we get it done every time, on time!

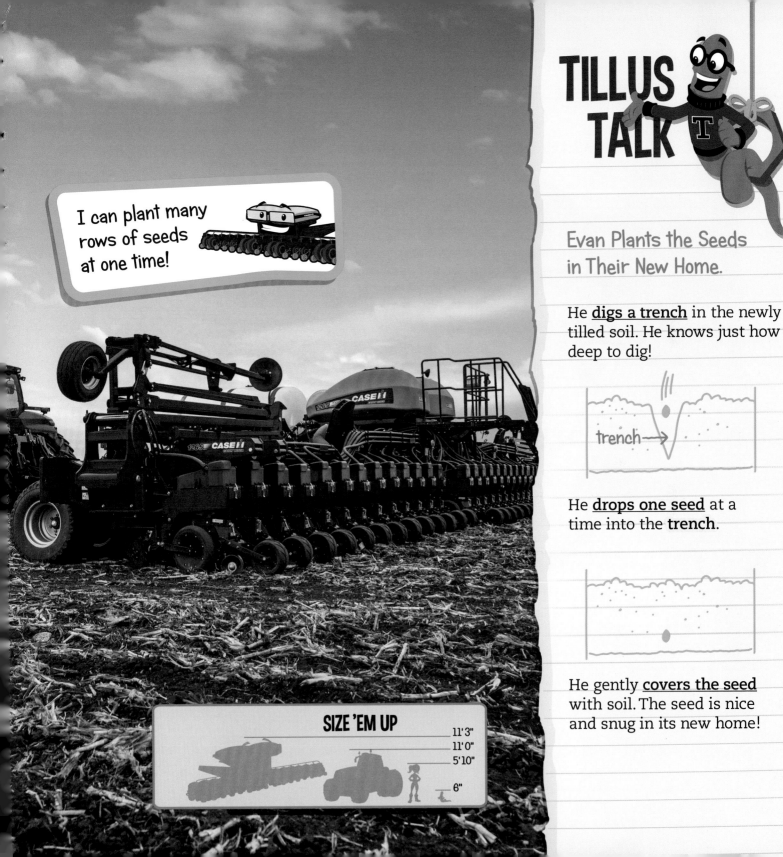

I can plant many rows of seeds at one time!

TILLUS TALK

Evan Plants the Seeds in Their New Home.

He **digs a trench** in the newly tilled soil. He knows just how deep to dig!

trench →

He **drops one seed** at a time into the **trench**.

He gently **covers the seed** with soil. The seed is nice and snug in its new home!

SIZE 'EM UP

11' 3"
11' 0"
5' 10"

6"

Summer on Happy Skies Farm is sunny and hot! My newly planted seeds are growing into little sprouts, and the fields are turning green! It is my job to protect these little sprouts so they can grow into healthy plants. It's time for me to check on them!

Warm, sunny weather helps Casey's plants grow. But if summer winds blow in cooler weather, the plants may grow too slowly. Or if the sun beats down on the fields for many weeks, the plants become hot and dry. Although Casey can't change the weather, she can help her plants make it through the long, hot summer.

sunny
81°

Protect the Plants!

Now that the seeds are planted, they need to be protected from bugs and weeds. Some bugs like to eat healthy plants. Weeds, which are a type of plant, steal food and water from the soil. But don't worry—these pests and weeds are no match for my team!

I love helping plants grow!

My name is Peter, and I help Casey protect the crops. My sprinklers give each plant its own little bodyguard!

Don't worry, plants. I will help protect you!

SIZE 'EM UP

12' 0"

5'10"

6"

TILLUS TALK

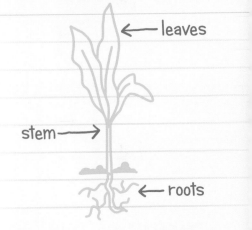

Plants Need Water and Food, Too!

Soil is not only the perfect home for plants, but it is also where the plants get their food and water.

← leaves

stem →

← roots

Roots act like a mouth and "suck up" food and water found in the soil.

Food and water travel up the **stem** to get to the other parts of the plant.

Leaves use food and water to help make energy from sunlight.

Now that's one busy plant!

WHERE CROPS

CORN

SOYBEANS

ARE GROWN

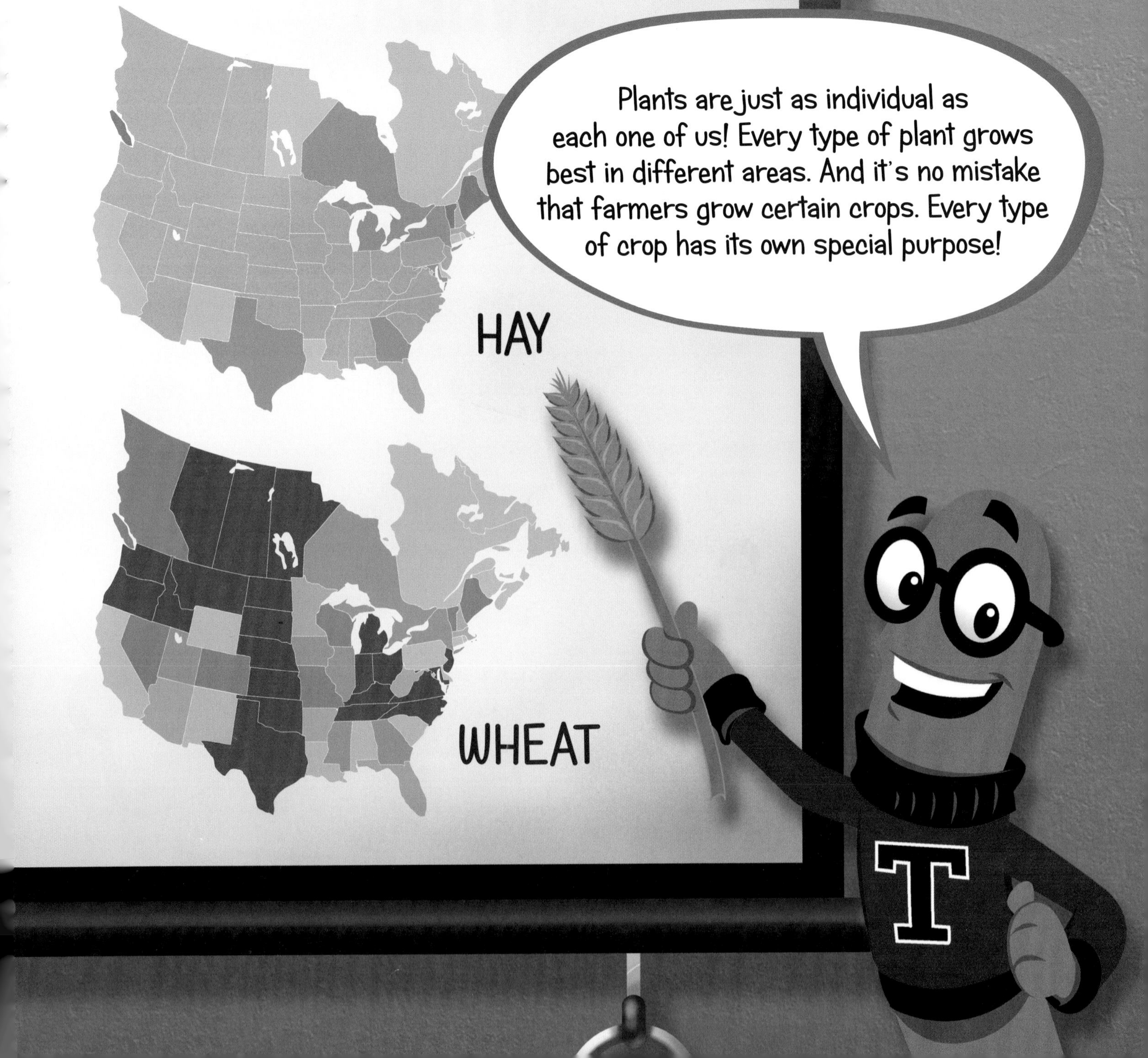
Plants are just as individual as each one of us! Every type of plant grows best in different areas. And it's no mistake that farmers grow certain crops. Every type of crop has its own special purpose!
HAY
WHEAT
T

WHEAT

Wheat is one of the building blocks of baking. Wheat flour is used in everything from making bread to cakes and cookies. There are different types of wheat, and each one is named after its color and the season it is grown in. A lot of wheat is grown in the middle part of the United States. In fact, there are so many wheat farmers in this area that it is called the "Bread Basket!"

CORN

Whether you eat it on the cob or in the form of a chip, corn is delicious! Even animals love corn. In fact, most corn is used to feed livestock. But did you know that corn can be turned into fuel, candles, crayons, and fireworks, too!

That's pretty a-MAIZE-ing!

GAS

CRAYON

YUM!

HAY

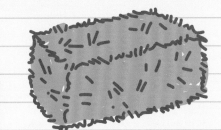

What do cows say when they see one another? "Hay!" Why? Because hay is a favorite food for farm animals like cows, horses, goats, and sheep. Some farmers grow hay to feed their own animals while other farmers sell the hay that they grow. Although people don't eat hay, it is an important crop for farmers to grow—cows and horses both agree!

SOYBEANS

Soybeans may be little, but they are in great big demand! That's because more people use soybean oil to cook with than any other oil. When this little bean isn't turned into oil, it is eaten in many different forms. Some people who cannot eat milk products, such as cheese and ice cream, eat soy products. Soy milk, soy ice cream, and tofu are just a few of the foods made from soybeans. The next time you have your picture taken, you can say, "Soy cheese!"

BAA.

The cool, crisp air and frosty mornings tell me that fall is here! I've been busy caring for my plants all summer long, and they have grown healthy and strong as a result. Now, I have to act fast and gather them before the winter weather sweeps in.

Let's get moving, team!

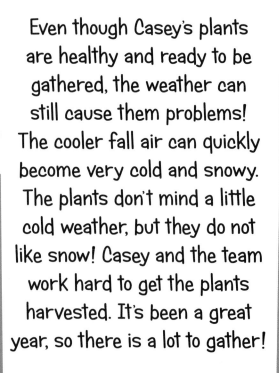

Even though Casey's plants are healthy and ready to be gathered, the weather can still cause them problems! The cooler fall air can quickly become very cold and snowy. The plants don't mind a little cold weather, but they do not like snow! Casey and the team work hard to get the plants harvested. It's been a great year, so there is a lot to gather!

cool
59°

Let's Harvest Corn!

All summer long, my corn plants have continued to grow. Now, they are taller than I am, and the stalks have ears of corn on them. That means it's time to harvest. We'd better get moving before the weather turns colder!

I'm Cody. After I cut down the stalk, I separate the tiny corn kernels from the rest of the plant. I save the kernels in a large bin. The rest of the plant gets chopped up and spread on the field behind me. I'm a one-stop shop!

CASE IH

CASE IH

That corn doesn't stand a chance!

All Done Growing!

Once the corn plant is fully grown, it has reached the end of its growing cycle.

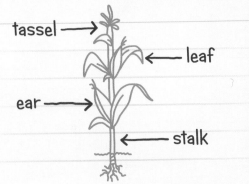

tassel →
← leaf
ear →
← stalk

A fully grown plant has a hairy **tassel** at the top of it and one or two **ears** of corn.

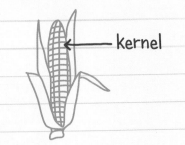

← kernel

An ear of corn is made up of little **kernels** attached to the cob. The kernels are the seeds of the corn plant!

SIZE 'EM UP

16'3"
5'10"
6"

Time for Grain!

Fall is busy because I have many different crops to harvest. In addition to corn, I grow grain. Both corn and grain crops need to be harvested around the same time. Thank goodness my team loves to work hard. Go, team!

I'm Kellie, and my job is to harvest the grain for Casey. I work just like Cody. Only I separate grain from the plant instead of corn kernels from the stalk.

CASE IH

CASE IH

The dark doesn't stop me!

The Difference is in the Headers.

Cody and Kellie do the exact same thing. So what makes them different?

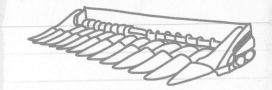

Cody has a **corn header**. The header looks like fingers that are spread out. The corn stalks are guided in between the fingers where Cody can easily cut them.

Kellie has a **grain header**. The header looks like many long combs that spin like a wheel. The combs push the plants toward Kellie while the header cuts them.

SIZE 'EM UP

16' 3"

5'10"

6"

Can't Forget the Hay!

Hay is harvested, or baled, several times throughout the summer and fall. That's good because I use it to feed my animals, and they love to eat fresh hay. It's a beautiful day, so I'd better get baling. We've got to make hay while the sun shines!

Hey, dudes! I'm Bailey! My job is to scoop up all of the freshly cut hay and turn it into nice, tight bales. Big Red is my main dude — he pulls me up and down the rows of cut hay. Gotta go! The hay waves are callin' my name!

Bailey is always looking to ride the best rows of hay, called windrows. Or as he calls them, hay waves! I've never seen a better baler than him!

CASE IH

CASE IH

Awesome hay wave!

CASE IH
LB334

SIZE 'EM UP

11'0"
10'3"
5'10"
6"

Hay! What's with the Shapes?

Farmers can bale hay into two different shapes: round or square.

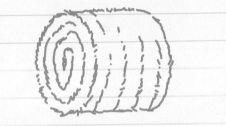

Round bales are much bigger than square bales. Their shape and size are good for farmers who have a lot of animals to feed.

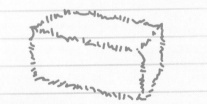

Square bales are dense. That means that the hay is packed tightly together. Square bales can fit neatly on top of one another and are easy to store in a barn.

Hurray! The crops are all harvested! And not too soon—it's snowing. My team and I have earned a break, but work on Happy Skies Farm never stops completely. In the winter, I take care of my team and get them ready for the next year. And then there are the animals! The animals need attention and care every day. I'd better go—can't keep the cows waiting!

Even though all of the crops are harvested, Casey continues to carefully watch the weather forecast. The animals depend on her to keep them safe and warm during harsh winter conditions. Casey also likes to know how much snow falls throughout the winter. Snow is good for the soil, and Casey is already planning for next spring!

Snow Can't Stop Me!

Everyone at Happy Skies Farm loves winter. Some of my tractors even have special attachments that they use in the snow. These tools help my team clear snow off roads and the farmyard. And they save me from having to shovel all that snow!

The snow is no laughing matter— unless it involves a snowball fight! Casey depends on me, Frankie, to make the farmyard safe for the equipment during snowy weather.

That's serious work!

The snow may be deep, but I won't get stuck!

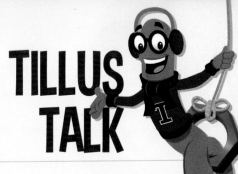

The Farmall is a Jack-of-all-Trades!

Frankie and Fern may be smaller than the other equipment, but they can do a lot of different jobs! No wonder Casey depends on them so much!

A **utility backhoe** attachment helps Frankie dig on the farm.

Fern helps Casey mow the grass along the road with a **rotary cutter** attachment.

SIZE 'EM UP

8'8"

5'10"

6"

Work, Work, Work!

Even though we are finished working in the fields, there's no time to rest! The animals need to be cared for everyday, all year long. Let's go, Fern. The cows are hungry!

Hi! I'm Fern! I love helping Casey take care of the animals. I use my bucket attachment to bring food to them. And when it's time to clean out the barn, my bucket scoops up dirty, stinky straw and carries it away.

I may be small, but I'm useful!

Come and get it!

Farming Year-Round.

There are many different jobs to do on a farm.

Farmers plant, grow, and harvest crops. The growing season begins in early spring and lasts through late fall.

Farmers take care of their animals. The animals need fresh food and water everyday!

Farmers make sure their equipment works properly. They can't run their farm without it!

SIZE 'EM UP

8'8"

5'10"

6"

CELEBRATE!
It has been a great year on the farm! My crops grew better than ever, giving me an extra big harvest. And my cows are healthy and happy. I'm very thankful for my team because I couldn't have done the work without them!
AWESOME JOB, TEAM!
CASE IH
CASE IH
CASE IH

GLOSSARY

ATTACHMENT

a tool that goes on a tractor and is used for special jobs

THE BREAD BASKET

an area in the United States where a lot of wheat is grown

CROPS

plants that a farmer grows

ENERGY

power that is used for work

FARMER

a person who owns or runs a farm

GOOD GROWING ENVIRONMENT

healthy soil that is tilled and prepared for planting

GROWING SEASON

the time it takes for a seed to grow into a full-grown plant

HARVEST

gathering of crops

HEADER

the part of a combine that gathers and cuts plants

SEED

the part of a plant that can grow into a new plant

SOIL

the layer of dirt that plants grow in

SPROUT

a young plant

TILL

the action of breaking up soil into small chunks

TRACTOR

a powerful machine that can be driven and is used on a farm

TRENCH

a ditch

WINDROW

hay that is cut and raked into rows

FUN FACTS!

Scientists can turn cow poop into usable energy!

1,000-year-old popcorn can still pop!

It is impossible for a pig to look up into the sky — its neck is too short!

Scientists in Antarctica use Steiger tractors to move
supplies across the frozen, snowy land!

CLUCK.

Birds are living dinosaurs. The chicken is the closest relative to the T-Rex!

During the winter of 1958, farmer John Steiger and his sons built the first
Steiger tractor in their barn!

One acre of soybeans can be turned into 82,368 crayons!

Like snowflakes, no two cows have exactly the same pattern of spots.
(They're MOO-nique!)

Earthworms naturally till the soil just by moving around. Go Tillus!

Octane Press, Edition 1.0, January 2015

©2015 CNH Industrial America LLC. All rights reserved. Case IH is a trademark registered in the United States and many other countries, owned by or licensed to CNH Industrial N.V., its subsidiaries or affiliates. www.caseih.com

Library of Congress Cataloging-in-Publication Data
ISBN: 1937747565 ISBN-13: 978-1-937747-56-5
1. Juvenile Nonfiction—Transportation—General. 2. Juvenile Nonfiction—Lifestyles—Farm and Ranch Life.
3. Juvenile Nonfiction—Lifestyles—Country Life. 4. Juvenile Nonfiction—Concepts—Seasons
Library of Congress Control Number: 2014943157

OCTANE
PRESS

octanepress.com
Printed in the USA